The Colors of the Sea

The Colors of the Sea
Copyright © 2023 by Gayle Paben
Published in the United States of America
ISBN Paperback: 978-1-960629-40-1
ISBN Hardback: 978-1-960629-54-8
ISBN eBook: 978-1-960629-41-8

All rights reserved. No part of this publication may be reproduced, stored in a retrieval system or transmitted in any way by any means, electronic, mechanical, photocopy, recording or otherwise without the prior permission of the author except as provided by USA copyright law.

The opinions expressed by the author are not necessarily those of ReadersMagnet, LLC.

ReadersMagnet, LLC
10620 Treena Street, Suite 230 | San Diego, California, 92131 USA
1.619. 354. 2643 | www.readersmagnet.com
Book design copyright © 2023 by ReadersMagnet, LLC. All rights reserved.

Cover design by Ericka Obando
Interior design by Daniel Lopez

GAYLE PABEN

Winner of two silver medals for her book *The Poetry of Animals*

ReadersMagnet, LLC

Prologue

This story takes place in the 1980's in Sarasota, Florida. Sarasota was a sleepy little town which was soon to turn into a growing city. Life at that time was a lot less full of the technology we use today. Most people were learning about the computer world and were communicating through email. Cell phones existed, but they were not yet being used by the average person. When a ten-year-old girl is forced to leave her home in a small town in Illinois, a new friend and a kindly old gentleman who loves to paint make her realize she has a lot to learn about the joys and hazard of Florida living and human nature. Things are not always as they seem...

Chapter 1

Casey had a knot in her stomach. She wasn't sure if she was nervous, hungry, or just tired. Her family's minivan pulled into The Blue Heron condo parking lot, and she stepped out of the van. Her leg muscles felt cramped after the long car ride, and she tried to stretch them out.

Cory, her 8-year-old younger brother, spotted several small lizards darting in and out of the shrubbery along the sidewalk.

"Oh, cool," he said, and immediately tried to catch one. When he grabbed at a small lizard, he caught it by the tail and was shocked when part of it broke off. He immediately dropped it and watched the missing tail part wiggle on the sidewalk.

"Oh gross," said Casey. She shuddered as she watched the tailless creature scurry into the nearest bush.

"It was an accident," Cory stammered, but his blue eyes stared fascinated as the tail still flopped on the sidewalk.

"Don't worry, the lizard will be fine," said a deep gentle voice. "That wiggling tail is just a decoy now to distract predators. It will take a few months, but it will grow a new one."

Casey looked toward the voice and saw a gray-haired man with eyes to match smiling down at them. He was carrying an easel, paint set, and a canvas.

"You must be the new managers' kids. I'm Mr. Kearns, and I've been helping out around here until your parents arrived. Welcome to Florida!"

Casey's parents stepped out from behind the silver van. Her dad shut the trunk, set his leather brief case down, and reached out to shake Mr. Kearns's hand.

"Nice to meet you, Mr. Kearns. I'm Michael Simms, and this is my wife, Kerry. I see you've already met Casey and Cory. They are not as excited about this new venture as my wife and I are."

"Is that right?" said Mr. Kearns smiling at the two children.

"It's a vacation spot not a home," Casey tossed her sun-streaked hair and looked at the ground so she wouldn't have to take a chance on her misty hazel eyes connecting with her mom or dad.

"My wife and I were thrilled to leave Illinois winters and escape our daily rat race. We thought my construction experience and Kerry's property management skills made this the perfect business opportunity. We have dreamed of living on Siesta Key since we found this area on our honeymoon. We thought Casey and Cory would be as excited as we are."

"You two can go look at the beach," said their mom. "Stay together and stay out of the water. We'll be with you in just a few minutes. We want to stop in the office and take a quick look around. Then we'll go eat and wait for the furniture movers to get here."

"Are you sure that's sand?" Cory said as the two children walked closer to the water.

"It does look more like snow," Casey replied. She had never seen the ocean or a white beach. She kicked off her sandals and gingerly placed her foot on the sand. She had almost burned her foot on the yellow sands of Michigan's Warren Dunes last summer. It had been a very hot day but certainly no hotter than this weather.

"It feels cool instead of hot," Cory said.

"And soft," Casey added. It felt like flour as it sifted between her toes.

Tow-headed Cory was immediately drawn to a young boy flying a blue and yellow kite that was making all sorts of dips and turns. Its rounded shape reminded Casey of an octopus with its kite tails as multiple arms.

Casey was drawn to the water. She wrinkled her freckled nose when she smelled a slight fishy odor. The immense size of the ocean overwhelmed her, and she suddenly felt lonely. She couldn't wait for the phone line and computer to be hooked up so she could email Jen, her best friend. Hopefully she would come visit soon. Casey gradually stepped backwards keeping her eye on the water when she felt something brush her leg.

Someone firmly grabbed her arm and a voice said, "Hey, you need to look where you are going!"

She turned and faced a boy who was about two inches taller than she was. He was shaking his brown curly hair staring at her. He looked thoroughly disgusted.

"What do you think you are doing grabbing my arm like that?" Casey snapped.

The brown eyes glared as he spoke, "Just look at what you almost did…"

Casey looked down. She saw that it was a yellow tape that had brushed her leg. Four stakes were placed in the ground and had orange flags tied to them. The stakes were surrounded by the tape. "What is it anyway?"

"I should have known, just another tourist who has no clue about the beach," the frowning face answered.

"For your information, I am not a tourist…although I wish I was just a tourist. Then I wouldn't have to come live where there are such rude people."

Casey felt a lump in her throat, and she struggled not to show the tears that were fighting their way to her eyes. She wished she was home with her friends, on her way to softball practice, cheerleading camp, or anywhere away from here. Mom and Dad hadn't even consulted her or Cory to discuss this life changing decision. It wasn't fair that she had been forced to leave her home, her friends, teammates, and school. She had been elected to Student Council and was planning on running for secretary in the fall. The first tear won and dribbled off her cheek.

The boy paused and then said in a softer tone, "Well I really didn't mean to hurt your feelings. It's just that I've lived on Siesta Key all my life. I get annoyed with people who come to visit but don't care about leaving the beach the way they found it. You almost stepped into a sea turtle's nest. You could have destroyed some of the eggs."

"Well, how was I supposed to know? We've only been here about twenty minutes," Casey sighed. She combed her fingers through her shoulder length hair, and gazed out across the water.

The boy's face began to relax, and the frown began to invert. "Are you really going to live here?"

"I'm afraid so," answered Casey.

"I'm sorry if I scared you," he said.

"It's okay," Casey responded, "I wouldn't have wanted to hurt the eggs."

"Good. I'm Matt Wilson. I live about three blocks from here with my mom and two older brothers. Our house isn't on the beach, but I spend most of my free time here."

"How long before they hatch?" asked Casey.

"The date is marked on the stakes when the nest was first found. It takes about two months or so. That means they could hatch in about a week. I'm keeping a close eye on the nest, because I want to be here when it happens. I'll come get you if you'd like. Where can I find you?"

Casey pointed back to The Blue Heron. "My parents will be managing the complex so just stop in at the office." She saw that her parents were waving at her.

"Just ask for Casey," she added.

She jogged back to get her brother and hoped that it was finally time to get something to eat. She was starving.

Chapter 2

The Blue Heron was a large twenty-five-year-old condo complex. Its location was perfect in that some of its units were on the beach side of the key and some were across the streets and faced the intercoastal waterway. Lounge chaises surrounded the pool near the office on the gulf side, and the intercoastal side offered a small fishing pier near a grassy barbeque area. Some of the residents were permanent, but many were snowbirds who enjoyed winter in Florida. Keeping the empty condos filled with holiday renters was to be a big part of Kerry's job.

The next few days were spent unpacking and organizing the Simms family's new home. Their unit was airy looking and in good condition, but the living space was much smaller than their Illinois house. There were no basements and not much closet space.

Their former home had both an attic and a finished basement. She had spent many hours playing pool and ping pong in her basement with friends. She remembered that The Blue Heron had a community center and wondered if she could talk her parents into adding a pool table and ping pong table. She would have to plan her strategy. She smiled as she thought how she would tell them that their guests needed something to do on those rainy days that they couldn't be on the beach.

"I'll win that argument," she smiled to herself.

"Where am I supposed to put all our kitchen supplies?" Casey's mom muttered.

"We could go back to Illinois and have all our space back," Casey couldn't resist commenting.

Kerry Simms shook her head and turned to look at her daughter. "We probably should talk more about a baby sitter."

"Come on Mom, I'm ten and a half years old, and you know I am responsible. I'll keep an eye on Cory. Our unit is only four doors down from the main office, so we're really close to you all the time. Besides, you have that little room off the office with the couch, TV, and small table. We can hang out there part of the day when we get tired of being in the condo."

"I suppose we could give it a try," her mom said. "There is such a gentle slope into the water, and the lifeguards are scattered across the beach. I guess all those years of swimming lessons should make me comfortable," she added.

"We'll be fine, I promise," Casey insisted.

Casey went to her room. Her yellow checked bedspread and white furniture seemed to work quite well in her sunlit room. Her stuffed animals seemed comfortable on the shelf dad had put up for her, so being surrounded by her favorite belongings did seem to improve her mood. On the other hand, e-mail from Jen told her that the softball team's record was 8 and 2. She was disappointed that they were managing just fine without her at second base.

It was after dinner, and Mrs. Simms was just getting ready to close the office for the day when a brown-haired boy opened the office door. Mrs. Simms thought he looked about eleven. "Hi, I'm looking for Casey."

Casey stepped out from the back room.

"The hatchlings…they've started coming out of the nest."

"Cory, come on. You'll want to see this too." Casey made the introductions and the three of them raced down to the beach to the orange flagged stakes.

Two volunteer workers were helping the fledglings emerge from the nest.

"Wow," said Cory, "there must be about a hundred eggs in that nest."

"The eggs look like little ping pong balls," Casey added.

"One of the most amazing things to me is that scientists believe the females come back to the spot where they hatched to lay their eggs. It is hard to imagine because turtles aren't even ready to lay eggs for more than 20 years, maybe even 50." Matt said.

"How in the world can they find it?" Casey asked.

"I'm not sure, but it is supposed to have something to do with the earth's magnetic fields."

Casey watched in awe as one by one, the two-inch-long black turtles emerged from the eggs and each one headed for the water. "How do they know what direction to go?"

"Instinct," answered Matt, "They should be okay right here. In some places, the lights of the condos are too bright, like down by the tennis courts. The hatchlings get disorientated and head in the wrong direction. They think it is the moonlight. Then the seagulls or raccoons have even more time to spot and eat them before they make it to the water."

The trio stayed at a good distance, but a crowd had begun to gather to enjoy this amazing vacation bonus. The baby turtles scurried to the water. The waves slapped them, and the breaking surf pushed them back toward the shore.

Casey frowned. "It's too hard for them to go into those waves."

"So far so good. They've made it to the water. If they don't swallow a plastic bag thinking it's a jellyfish, or get into a polluted area, they might have a chance. Only about one in one thousand actually survives twelve years to become an adult sea turtle."

The struggling hatchlings did not appear to be discouraged by the wave action and continued to work their way into the sea. The crowd started to drift apart as the little black disks bobbed and finally disappeared into the water. Casey was impressed not only with Matt's knowledge, but that he had remembered to come get her. The sight of all those hatchlings trying to scamper on those short little legs to the edge of the water was a sight she would never forget.

"Thanks for coming to get me. I'm glad I got to watch, she said. Casey knew she had made her first Florida friend.

Chapter 3

Casey was tired of watching television. She and Cory grabbed cokes and a bag of pretzels and went outside to the picnic table where a gentle breeze offered some relief from the stifling heat.

"Here comes JR again," Casey sighed as she watched a teenage boy from the complex bound down the stairs with his metal detector clutched in his hand.

"I see him go out every day," Cory added, "I wonder what he finds out there. Do you think he'd let me go with him?"

"You could ask, but he doesn't seem that friendly to me." Casey replied.

Cory took off running after JR. The thin black-haired teenager glanced over his shoulder and picked up his pace. Cory took the hint, hung his head slightly, and walked slowly back toward his sister.

"Maybe he didn't see you," Casey said as he approached her. She was relieved to see Matt heading toward the shaded picnic table near the office where they were sitting. At least there was a gentle breeze.

"Got any ideas?" Casey asked. "It's too hot and we're bored."

Casey offered Matt some pretzels, and he sat down with them at the table.

"Do you want to play tennis?" Matt asked.

"Are you kidding?" said Casey as she wiped the sweat out of her eyes. "I can barely breathe now."

"There are some great sandcastles and sculptures down on the beach," said Matt. "There's a four-foot-high castle, an alligator, and a dolphin. You might learn some great tricks for building your own castles. Do you want to go take a look?"

Casey opened her mouth to answer but let out a scream instead.

"Ouch! That hurts!"

She jumped up from the table and looked at her legs which were stinging terribly now. Her legs were covered up to her knees with a swarm of little red ants.

"Fire ants!" Matt yelled. He started to help Casey slap at them and then shouted,

"Quick! Jump in the pool."

Casey ran about 30 steps and jumped into the pool.

Cory ran toward the office, and Dad was already there as Casey dragged herself out of the pool. Tears were running down her cheeks.

"I hate it here," Casey said as her dad helped her finish brushing off the insects.

"I didn't even know they were there, and then it was like they all stung at the same time! It's almost like they had a leader who gave them a signal that said 'Get Casey!'"

"Fire ants are known to do that," said Matt quietly. "I should have warned you to be on the lookout for them. They have a nasty little venom they inject, and soon you will have little white blisters all over your legs."

Casey couldn't help herself. She had to count. "Just great, eighty-three bites."

Mom came out with a paste made from baking soda and water. "I don't know if this will work, but Mr. Kearns said it would help take out the sting."

"At least it doesn't seem that you are allergic to the ant venom," Dad said. "Some people have severe reactions. They have trouble breathing and need to go to the hospital."

"This stinging is plenty bad enough," said Casey tossing her head in the air. "What other hazard do I need to know about this place?" Casey muttered as she got up from the picnic table and walked toward the condo.

"I don't think she'll be too crazy about the alligators, rattlesnakes, or palmetto bugs either," she heard Matt whisper to Cory. She glanced over her shoulder and saw that Matt had a sheepish grin on his face.

✶ ✶ ✶ ✶ ✶ ✶

Casey woke early the next morning. She had trouble sleeping, and she stared at the little white blisters. She decided to take a walk on the beach before breakfast to get her mind off the bites. The water was calm and glistened in the sunlight. The beach was dotted with walkers and joggers. Sandpipers darted in and out of the water. They paused occasionally to poke their pointed beaks into the wet sand.

As she walked along the edge of the beach, a large blue heron stood watching Mr. Kearns who had waded into the water and was casting his line. "This is Old Hubert," he said looking at Casey and nodding at the heron. "He's going to try and steal his breakfast from me. I'm not going to make it easy for him," he said as he rearranged the net covering bucket. "How are those ant bites this morning?"

"I think the baking soda did help," said Casey. "Thanks for the tip, but I hope I won't need it ever again."

"Well, let's hope you never get that many at a time. Even one or two bites can be annoying," Mr. Kearns sympathized. "Did you notice the dolphins out there this morning?" Mr. Kearns asked.

"Where?" Casey asked raising her hand above her eyes to cut the glare.

"Keep looking about twenty yards out. They were just straight ahead of you, so look south about ten feet. I believe it is a bottlenose dolphin. Do you see its short thick snout? It also has a curved mouth which makes it look as though it is smiling. They are intelligent creatures for sure."

"And fun to watch! I didn't expect to see dolphins this close to shore," Casey whispered as she spotted two dolphins. She didn't think that they could hear her, but she didn't want to scare them away. She stood and watched them surface and dive.

"It looks like they are playing," Casey noted.

"That's exactly what they're doing," Mr. Kearns agreed. "They love following the boats and jumping in their wakes. I swear they'd talk to us in English if they could."

Casey watched the dolphins until they no longer were visible. "Thanks for pointing them out," she said as she headed down toward Point of Rocks at the south end of the beach.

Matt was coming out of the water with another boy. He introduced Casey to his older brother, Sam, who was headed toward the volleyball courts to meet some of his friends. "Nice to meet you, but I'm late for my game. See you around."

"How are the bites this morning?" Matt inquired.

"Don't remind me," Casey stated, "I'm trying not to think about them."

Matt lifted his mask and said, "Do you like to snorkel? There were some neat schools of fish out there this morning."

"I'm a decent swimmer, and I have used a mask and snorkel. There wasn't much reason to use it in a pool."

"Here… you can try mine. I'm ready for a rest anyway," Matt said. He rinsed all the pieces, adjusted the straps on his fins, and handed them to her. "Be careful where you step. Some of those rocks are sharp, and stay away from oyster beds. They are brutal."

Casey put on the mask, snorkel, and flippers and walked out on the rocks until she found a place to step down into the water. She waded a short distance, which was tricky with the flippers, until she was deep enough that she could swim. The water was clear this morning, and it felt good. She was still adjusting to learning to swim with so much salt in the water; but for some reason, swimming in the ocean on a calm day was almost easier than a pool—except for the salt taste. She stopped swimming and just sort of floated on top of the water. She was fascinated when she saw her first school of fish. It was amazing how they all turned at the same time. All of a sudden she swallowed some water and started coughing.

"Are you okay?" Matt yelled to her.

Casey had to come back to shore and struggled to catch her breath.

"I'm fine," she gasped. "I couldn't help it. When I saw all the fish, it made me giggle."

"You're not allowed to giggle when you are snorkeling," Matt said as he shook his head and laughed.

Casey finally stopped coughing. "I'm definitely going to have to practice."

"Could I ask you a something?" Matt said seriously.

"What?" asked Casey.

"Do you really hate it here?" asked Matt.

"Not all the time," Casey sighed, "not this morning anyway. Let's go see if Old Hubert the heron got any of Mr. Kearn's fish."

They picked up the snorkeling equipment and headed back up the beach.

Chapter 4

Mr. Kearns had packed up his fishing gear and was gazing out across the water as Matt and Casey approached.

"Did Old Hubert get his breakfast this morning?" Matt asked.

Mr. Kearns grinned. "He managed to get a small flounder that I intended to throw back, because it was too small to keep."

"What are you looking at?" Casey inquired.

"The color of the sea," Mr. Kearns responded. "What colors do you see this morning?"

"Blue, I guess," Matt responded

"Look again," Mr. Kearns encouraged.

"Well, I see a dark blue line across the horizon, and then I see some bluish green near it."

"What about you, Casey?"

"I see royal blue broken up by the white caps that look like shimmery white crystals. It looks more aqua up here near the beach where it is shallow."

"That's better," Mr. Kerns added. "I need to get my water colors out this morning and see if I can imitate Mother Nature's palette. I've always been fascinated by the amazing combinations of color. I would say the horizon looks ultramarine blue, fades into a phthalo blue, and becomes turquoise close to shore. The sky is cerulean blue which of course affects the colors of the sea. The sea has many moods, almost like a personality. Sometimes it is peaceful and serene, and other times it is downright angry. The colors of the sea are like each new day…always changing and full of surprises."

Casey stared at the water, trying to imagine how it could have a personality. A laughing gull's cry interrupted the silence.

"All this fresh air is making me hungry," he added. "I think I'll head back to see if I can quiet the old rumblings in this stomach of mine."

As the three of them walked toward the Blue Heron, they could see Casey's mom waving at them to hurry up.

"What a day this has been!" she began. "Mrs. Labelle's cat got out and we haven't been able to find it. The cable installers are doing some retrofitting, and Mr. Turner fell and sprained his ankle. I found someone to take him to the Walk-In Clinic, and now Mrs. Schmitt has a problem with the plumbing in her bathroom. She is insisting someone come look at it immediately. Kevin had to go to Tampa this morning. I know you were helping with repairs before we came,

Mr. Kearns. I am begging you to look at Mrs. Schmitt's problem so we can calm her down. The plumber can't get here until tomorrow. Besides, Kevin could probably fix it if he were here.

"Mrs. Schmitt, huh. That old gal and I have had a few run-ins in the past. She doesn't think any of our recycling rules are meant for her, or any other rule or common courtesies for that matter."

"Please, Mr. Kearns," pleaded Kerry Simms, "she won't even be there. She has theater tickets this afternoon. We'll pay you for your time, and we'll have you come down to our next barbeque on the beach."

"Now it's bribery is it?" Mr. Kearns grinned. "That steak last night smelled great. Oh all right, I'll take your bribe and see if there is anything I can do. Just let me grab a bite to eat. Be sure she is gone for the afternoon."

"Great," said Kerry, and she handed him the keys.

****

Casey and Matt picked up badminton rackets and were hitting the birdie back in forth next to the parking lot. Matt whipped one hard, and it flew near the back door of the cable man's van. Casey ran over to pick it up when a voice yelled, "Hey, you kids need to stay away from my equipment! Get away from there, now."

Casey looked up to see a black-haired, medium-built man glaring down at her from the railing on the third floor.

"We're not going to bother your truck, mister," she hollered back as she picked up the feathered object and held it up for him to see.

"Find somewhere else to play," he shouted back.

"What a grouch," Matt whispered as she came back near him, and they sat back down at the picnic table.

"I need food," Casey said and headed into their room next to the office. They made peanut butter sandwiches, grabbed some grapes, and settled on a nice quiet game of checkers at the picnic table while they munched their sandwiches.

Mr. Kearns was back before two and handed the key back to Kerry Simms.

"No panic. It was just a simple problem. I changed the flapper in the tank. It's fixed. Mrs. Schmitt can relax for once."

"We owe you. Thanks." Mrs. Simms smiled. "Now if we could just find that darn cat."

"I'm off duty," said Mr. Kearns as he picked up his box of watercolors and his easel.

Just then the phone rang and Mrs. Simms gave a thumbs up. "Found the cat! Whew…" she added.

Cory noticed JR going to the beach again and this time was determined to tag along.

"JR, can I come see what you find today?" he asked softly.

"Sorry. How can I meet any girls on the beach asking me about what I'm finding if I've got a little kid tagging along with me?" he muttered and hurried toward the beach.

Cory's shoulder sagged.

"Just ignore him, Cory. He's more interested in girls than what he's finding anyway."

Mr. Kearns had overheard the conversation and walked back toward them.

"Don't let him get to you," he said. "JR's parents sort of shipped him down here for the summer to stay with his aunt. His mom was having surgery. They thought it would be easier for him and everyone if he spent the summer in Sarasota. A summer at the beach sounded good, but he does not want to be here."

"That we can understand," Casey stated.

"He's not a bad kid, just a little on the angry side. I don't think he's made any friends here."

Four hours had passed when the quiet complex was broken by a shriek.

"Call the police." screamed Mrs. Schmitt. "I've been robbed!"

Chapter 5

Mrs. Simms invited Matt to stay for dinner, so he called his mom for permission. Casey couldn't remember a more silent time at the dinner table.

"It's not fair, Mom. You know Mr. Kearns would never steal," Casey blurted out.

"I know. Everyone likes and respects him,"

"Except Mrs. Schmitt," Casey commented.

"No one is going to think he did it. The problem is there is no sign of forced entry," her mom added.

"It's still not fair! He was doing you a favor," Casey complained.

Kerry Simms looked as pale as she had when she had heard Mrs. Schmitt's first scream. "I should never have asked him to go in there without going with him."

Michael Simms squeezed his wife's hand. "Whoever did this was only interested in cash, and they got less than a hundred dollars. Mrs. Schmitt had valuable items, but they weren't touched."

"Mrs. Schmitt almost looked happy when she found out that Mr. Kearns was the last known person to enter her apartment," said Casey.

"I think she had a smirk on her face," Matt added.

Casey put her fists under her chin as she rested her elbows on the table. "Well, that cable guy was in a lot of units today."

"He sure didn't want us anywhere near his truck," Matt said.

"We can't start blaming people, Casey. You know that." her dad responded.

"Mrs. Schmitt didn't have any trouble blaming Mr. Kearns," said Casey.

Casey and Matt cleared the table and then walked down to the edge of the water.

They watched the pelicans fly in V formation. Several broke from the flock and did a dive bomb for their prey in the water.

"I never get tired of watching the pelicans," Matt said.

"That one had a successful dive. Look at the fish he caught," Casey added as they watched the pelican bob in the water with its prize sticking out of its mouth.

"The color of the sea is grayish brown tonight," said Matt.

"Even the sea is sad," Casey sighed. "Maybe there is something to this personality thing with the sea."

She couldn't help but notice all the birds flying mostly in the same direction. "Where are they going?"

"They're headed for their rookeries for the night before it gets dark," Matt stated. "There are a lot of mangrove islands around here, and a few are their favorites where they go before the light is gone."

"I don't know anything about the mangroves," said Casey. "We sure don't have trees that look like that in Illinois!"

"The birds love to hang-out on the mangrove island for the night," Matt said.

"Oh so that is why you see so many birds flying in the same direction at this time of the evening. They know exactly where they are going," Casey commented.

Matt added, "The mangroves are really important to the eco system. Think of them as a nursery for all the tiny fish, mollusks, and crustaceans. They can hide from the big fish in all those tangled roots. They would not survive without the protection of the mangroves."

"Wow…nature is amazing," Casey said. "Never really thought that much about it at home."

"Those dark gray clouds are coming fast. See where they are touching the water out there. That means it is already raining, and it will be here soon. I'd better get home," Matt stated.

****

Casey couldn't sleep. She pulled the covers over her head to block the sound of the rain that was pelting against her window.

"Aagggh!" a loud scream came from the kitchen.

She recognized her mother's voice and jumped out of bed.

"I just turned on the light and a huge cockroach scurried across the floor in front of me." Kerry Simms stammered.

"Really, Mom, it's just a palmetto bug." Casey couldn't resist. "Welcome to Florida!"

"Palmetto bug might be the nice name for it; but it's really a cockroach, and it is in my kitchen."

Michael Simms had entered the room quietly, exterminated the object of the commotion with the heel of his shoe, and was picking up the squished insect with a paper towel. "I guess we know why we're paying a monthly bill to the pest control people," he commented. "Nowhere is perfect, I guess, but you'll have to admit this is close."

Casey rolled her eyes and headed back to bed.

****

The next morning Dad came to the breakfast table with a strange object in his hand. It had a handle like a broom and a scoop-shaped bottom with a metal netting covering it.

"What is that?" Cory asked inquisitively.

"This is what we call a Florida snow shovel. They tell me it is great for finding shark's teeth, and the best place to find them is in the Venice area. It just so happens that I have an errand to run down that way, and I thought you might want to do some hunting. I could spare an hour stop if you want to ride along with me."

"Might as well," Casey said. "It will help get my mind off Mr. Kearns for a while."

Casey was surprised when they arrived at Venice Beach to see how different it was from Siesta Key. The sand was not the white quartz beach of Siesta Key, and it had a lot more shells. It was not nearly as soft. She noted the greenish-brown color of the water with the heavy overcast sky. She wondered how the beaches could be so close and yet so different.

She picked up a piece of abalone shell and studied the beautiful pink and purple colors. Mr. Kearns and Matt had both been teaching her the names of some of the various shells. She picked up a few shells that she wanted to take with her. She could recognize scallops coquinas, bear claws, jingles, and conchs; but she had a lot to learn. She loved the beautiful colors and shapes and how different they all were. The shells with bright pink and purple colors were her favorite.

"Hmm…" she thought, "more color of the sea!"

Cory was already digging, and after about five minutes let out a whoop. "Got one!"

Sure enough, the half inch long black tooth was pretty much intact, and the search was on. They dug the shovel into the sand and sifted out the sand.

"I feel like I'm panning for gold," Casey laughed.

"I think it's pretty cool," Cory said.

At the end of their hour, they had found seven teeth between them. They were various shades of brown, black, or gray. The smallest ones were only about an eighth of an inch long and their main treasure was close to an inch. Casey collected a small variety of shells, and she placed them in a separate bucket.

"Not a bad start," their dad said as they put their things back in the car. "Next time we'll try Caspersen Beach down the road a little. I hear that's even better for shark's teeth."

"I wonder where they all come from," Casey thought out loud as she threw her towel in the trunk.

"Well, I know that shark continually shed their teeth and grow new ones," her dad said. "I read that a shark can produce about 29,000 teeth in its lifetime, but some of these teeth have been around for thousands of years. Why they happen to wind up in this area I have no clue."

The Colors of the Sea

When they arrived at the Blue Heron, Casey called Matt and told him to come see their shark teeth. When he got there, they pulled the shells and shark teeth out and set them on newspaper on the picnic table. Mr. Kearns walked toward them about the same time JR and the metal detector reached the picnic table area.

"Which part of the beach are you headed to today, JR?" asked Mr. Kearns.

"I haven't been to the north end for about a week. Guess I'll start off in that direction," came the reply. "Nothing else to do."

"Well, Cory would love to tag along and keep you company," Mr. Kearns added.

"Yeah, I didn't mean to be so tough on you Cory," JR said. "I'm just sort of desperate here trying to meet some chicks," JR offered a weak smile.

"You never know…might even make it easier." Mr. Kearns winked.

"Maybe another day, if it's okay with you."

Cory was slightly embarrassed and nodded his head

"Wish there were more kids your age staying here this summer, JR," Mr. Kearns added. "What about the volleyball courts?"

"I stink at volleyball," JR replied. "If I go down to watch, they ask me to play. Then they roll their eyes because I'm lousy at the sport.

Afraid I don't make much of an impression. Metal detecting is easier on the ego. See you later."

As he walked away Casey whispered to Matt, "I guess he's not so bad. I'd be pretty grumpy if I didn't have you or Cory to hang out with."

Mr. Kearns stopped and examined their treasures.

"I'm pretty sure most of these shells do not have any living creatures still inside them, which is a good thing," Mr. Kearns noted. "I know you wouldn't have wanted to hurt the living ones, but nothing smells worse than the ones that die after you have collected them. You still might want to have your mom help you wash them with a bleaching solution, 50/50 water and bleach. Then if you really want them to look good, you might want to polish them with a little mineral oil. Do you remember the names?"

"Well, I know I have a few bivalves, not connected, I'm afraid. But I also found a few olives, bear claws, scallops, but I don't know what this one is…"

Casey stretched up her hand and Mr. Kearns took the shell.

"Oh, that is a whelk," Mr. Kearns responded.

Casey looked up at the gray eyes and said, "I'm sorry you got blamed for the trouble yesterday."

"Well, that certainly is one of those surprises that I mentioned that each day brings. Surprises are not always pleasant… that is for sure." He paused and then added, "Now don't you worry that pretty little head of yours. I know I didn't do anything wrong, and these things have a way of sorting themselves out."

"Well, I hope it happens soon. It's not fair to have Mrs. Schmitt blabbing and complaining the way she is."

"Well, I'm afraid that reaction isn't one of the surprises. Life is too short for grudges; but for some reason, she and I have those occasional clashes. I can't believe she really thinks I would steal her money."

Mr. Kearns shrugged his shoulders and headed back toward his unit.

Chapter 6

Casey woke up to the sunshine warming her bed. She stretched and walked over to the window. The beach had been raked clean by the tractors as it was every morning. Joggers and walkers skimmed the water's edge trying to take advantage of the fresh morning air. A parasail trailed behind a large motor boat, and a few white sails appeared on the horizon. The beach was coming to life. The water was a beautiful shade of aquamarine. "A new color for Mr. Kearns's palette," Casey whispered.

Another color caught her eye. This is one she hadn't noticed before. She knew that a green flag meant it was safe to be in the water, and red meant stay out usually due to undertows and rip tides.

"Dad, what does the blue flag on the beach mean?" Casey asked as she walked into the kitchen. She popped some bread in the toaster.

"It usually means that something there is some dangerous marine life in the water. It could mean sharks, jellyfish, stingrays, or something like that. Stay out of the water," her dad cautioned.

"No problem. The fire ant incident was enough for me to take creature warnings seriously," Casey responded.

Cory had wandered into the kitchen.

"Can we run down to the lifeguard stand and ask him about the flag color?" Casey asked.

"Sure," their mom answered, "but I need for you to run a quick errand first."

A delivery was made to the wrong unit. I called Mrs. Miller to see if she was home. I told her you'd run this up there for her."

Casey was anxious to get down to the beach, so she grabbed the package and headed for the elevator. The cable installers were working on the third floor where Casey was headed. She realized she was going to have to walk right passed them to get to Mrs. Miller. She considered going back down a flight and coming up the stairs at the other end, but decided she was in too much of a hurry. She avoided the eyes of the worker who had yelled at her and Matt the other day, but she felt he was staring her and she couldn't wait to get passed him. "I still don't trust him," she thought to herself.

Mrs. Miller thanked her for running the package up to her and offered her a chocolate chip cookie for her trouble. Casey munched on it as she took the longer route down the stairs to avoid meeting the cable workers again. As she turned the corner on the second floor, she noticed JR pause and stoop down. She started to say, "Good morning," but he hadn't noticed her and hurried toward the stairwell in the opposite direction. "He really isn't as much of a jerk as I thought he was in the beginning," Casey thought.

"It's about time," Cory said when she got back and the two of them raced down to the lifeguard stand.

"We've had two people stung by stingrays this morning," a bronzed young lifeguard told them. "We sent them both to the hospital just to be safe. You two know about doing the stingray shuffle, don't you?"

Casey and Cory shook their heads. "Not really."

"Well, when you wade in the water, you need to learn to push the sand with your toes and shuffle your feet, because stingrays like to bury themselves in the sand. The stingrays will feel the vibration and move away from you. If they get startled, they snap up a nasty barb at the end of their tail. It will hurt, and I mean bad." The lifeguard continued, "At first it feels as though you stepped on a something sharp like a nail, then the poison takes effect. Talk about pain! A spine from a mature stingray can be several inches long. It has a serrated barb and is coated with a toxin. I hope you never find out what it feels like, but unfortunately, I know about it first-hand. You need to be especially careful from May through October,"

"Thanks for talking to us. I don't think we'll be spending any time in the water today!"

Matt was waiting for them when they got back to the office. He nodded at JR as he walked passed him.

"I wanted to make sure you knew about the stingrays," he said.

"Wild horses couldn't drag me into that water today," Casey stated.

Matt and Casey started a game of Mancala on the picnic table when a flock of noisy green parrots squawked overhead and settled in the cabbage palms near in front of the entrance to the business office.

"Whoever heard of wild parrots?" Casey said.

Mr. Kearns joined them at the table. "I don't know where they came from," he said, "but the flock seems to get bigger and noisier every year. I've seen them in Bradenton, at the airport, and down by the bay. I always wonder if it is the same flock, or if there are more of them now."

The squawking flock had rested long enough and took off, turning heads of tourists as they flew.

Matt kicked off his tennis shoe and tried to remove several bothersome sandspurs that he had picked up on his shortcut through one of the few remaining vacant lots. They were stuck to his shorts.

"These things are so annoying," he complained.

Mr. Kearns handed him a comb and said, "Here try this. It's a little trick I learned."

"Thanks," said Matt as he combed them off his shorts.

"Well, I needed to get out my paints this morning," Mr. Kearns winked. "What do you think?"

Matt and Casey looked at the beautiful deep colors of his newly created seascape.

"I couldn't help but notice the aquamarine color this morning. I think you captured the color perfectly."

"Pretty soon you'll be like me. You won't be able to look at the water without thinking about color," Mr. Kearns winked.

A squad car pulled into the parking lot and they saw an officer walking toward the office. "Now what?" Casey wondered out loud.

Kerry Simms looked drained as she escorted the officer to Mrs. Kelly's apartment. She stopped by the table on her way back and sat down looking exasperated.

"It's happened again. Mrs. Kelly went grocery shopping for an hour this morning, and she came home to find that someone had stolen her coin jar and some cash she had hidden in a drawer. Nothing else is missing, just about fifty dollars. And again…no sign of forced entry."

Mr. Kearns shook his head and said, "I know this will really upset her. She has been nervous living alone since her niece moved out."

"There must have been plenty of people here that saw you painting on the beach this morning, Mr. Kearns. At least no one will be able to suspect you this time," said Casey.

"Thank goodness for small favors, but that certainly doesn't help Mrs. Kelly. I'd better check on her," Mr. Kearns replied. He picked up his painting and supplies and headed toward the stairwell.

"That crabby old cable guy was here again today," Casey commented.

"You heard your dad. We can't go blaming people," was the expected comment from her mom.

****

Casey woke up to a new color on the beach…silver. "What in the world?" she thought. As she peered out her window, it took a while for the sight she was seeing to register. The edge of the water had clumps of silver scattered along its edge. She walked out the front door and toward the water. The smell confirmed that something was wrong. Dead fish lined the shore, and she watch the seagulls pick at the lifeless forms. "That can't be a very healthy breakfast," Casey thought. When she got closer to the water, Casey's throat began to feel irritated. She began to cough and walked back to the office.

Mr. Kearns was already in the office speaking with her mom. "It's an outbreak of red tide."

"What is red tide?" Casey asked.

"It stinks out there," Cory commented as he walked in the door.

"That's because red tide is a toxic algae bloom," Mr. Kearns continued. "It looks more brownish than red when you see it in Florida waters. When it blooms, it gives off a toxic odor that can irritate your throat and make you cough. It can kill the fish and other creatures of the sea."

"What about the dolphins?" Cory asked.

"And the manatees?" Casey wanted to know. She was still hoping to see her first one.

If the bloom lasts for a long time, it can affect and possibly kill them too. Hopefully, this outbreak won't be around for long."

"What will our guests do if they can't stand to be outside?" Mrs. Simms asked.

"Well, the closer they get to the water, the more it will bother them. I'm always amazed how you hear people coughing, and you know it is annoying them; but they are not about to miss out on their vacations. They simply go inside to the air conditioning when they can't stand to be around it anymore. Neither of you two have asthma do you?"

Casey and Cory shook their heads.

"Well, try to think of activities away from the beach area for a few days."

Matt walked in the door with a grumpy look on his face.

"Mr. Kearns just explained to us about red tide," Casey informed him. "You forgot to warn me about this too."

Matt shrugged his shoulders. "I hate red tide," was his only comment.

Chapter 7

The next day brought a front that at least carried the odor out to sea instead of inland. Cory and Matt were restless and had already tired of watching movies.

Michael Simms walked in the office. "Guess who is all caught up. I think I'd like to take a little trip out to Myakka State Park. Alligators anyone?"

Screeches and scrambling began. Matt called home, and in twenty-five short minutes, the three children jumped into the van armed with coolers, picnic baskets, cameras, and binoculars. The thirty-minute drive passed quickly with spirited disagreements about how many alligators they would see.

Shortly after they entered the entrance to the park, they approached a small bridge where a few people had gathered. They were shading their eyes and pointing.

The car doors all opened and slammed shut as they all hopped out.

"I've only been here a couple of times," Matt commented, "and the last time it was so cold, we only saw two gators all day."

"I don't see any," said Cory.

"Do you see that log-like thing floating over there?" his dad asked.

"Yeah," Cory replied.

"That's number one."

"It doesn't look real. It is floating so slowly," Casey said.

They walked to the other side of the bridge and noticed a six-foot gator sunning itself on a log. It was only about fifteen feet away from them. It slipped into the water and started swimming toward the bridge.

Casey grabbed her camera and got a great shot of just a pair of eyes.

"He's staring right at me," she giggled.

Cory started to bound down the muddy ramp next to the water when his dad shouted, "Cory…stop!"

"I just wanted a closer look," he stammered.

"This isn't a zoo, Cory, and there are no bars to protect you."

"Or him," Casey laughed.

"He doesn't look as though he could move very fast," Cory muttered.

"Not true. Even though I've never seen it, I've read that alligators can run up to 30 miles per hour for short distances," his dad said.

"That's hard to imagine," Matt said.

"Why aren't you allowed to at least just feed them from the bridge?" Casey asked.

"It would be too dangerous. They would lose their fear of humans and start looking at them as a food source."

The next stop was the bird walk. The wooden deck extended way out into the marshland. They watched the long-legged birds wade through the grass hunting for their meals.

Using the park signs, they identified the moorhens, a small blue heron, a great white egret, and even saw several sandhill cranes.

"They are so big," Casey said. "I love their red heads!"

"They really are beautiful creatures, and we're lucky to see them. They are still on the endangered animal list," her dad added.

"My favorite bird to watch is the anhinga." Matt said as he pointed to one that looked as though it was drip drying its wings. "It swims fast under water to catch its prey but doesn't have the oil to protect it that most birds have. That is why it hangs its wings out in the sun to dry."

"I like the way they swim with that long snaky neck sticking out of the water," Cory added.

"Well, not being a real snake fan, they're not exactly my favorite; but I do like to watch them sun themselves," said Casey.

The last treat of the day was a trip on Upper Myakka Lake in the world's largest airboat. The ranger told them that there were approximately 800 alligators in the lake.

"I can't believe there are fishermen walking around in that water. Are they crazy?" Casey inquired.

Mr. Simms shook his head. I guess they must know what they are doing. They must avoid feeding times which I think is late afternoon. I was told the fishermen never wear their catches on their belts. But I sure wouldn't feel comfortable walking around in that water knowing that 800 gators were looking for dinner somewhere."

"Number twenty-one," Casey said as they crossed over the bridge on the way out of the park.

"That might be the same one we saw this morning," Matt said.

"No, I got a good look at his eye this morning. I think this is a different one," Casey giggled.

When they arrived at the Blue Heron, they went straight to their mom's office to fill her in on all the details of the day.

"I sure wish I could have been there," she smiled. "Sounds like a missed a great day." After a few seconds she added, "Oh, Casey, how would you like to earn a quick ten dollars?"

"What do I have to do?"

Mrs. Swenson went to visit her niece in Clearwater and isn't going to be home until late. She wanted you to feed her dog and take him for a walk. She said you have played with Chester a few times and thought you would be comfortable with him."

"Oh, I love that little dog. He's that cute Westie, a West Highlander terrier…not a problem."

"She said she'd leave a key under one of the flower pots outside her door. I think she said the purple one. Her unit number is 208."

"I'll go with you," Matt offered.

Matt and Casey walked up the stairs to the second floor and started down the corridor. Mrs. Swenson had quite a collection of pots outside her door. "Hope mom remembered the right color," Casey said.

Matt lifted the purple pot and picked up the key.

A very friendly bark met them at the door, and Matt and Casey stooped down to pet Chester. They laughed and enjoyed all the licks and kisses. He scooted under the chair and ran around the apartment in circles for about three minutes. He finally settled down to eat the food they poured into his dish.

Casey grabbed the leash. "Ready to go for a walk, boy?"

Again, Chester ran in circles around the dining room table for another two minutes before they could catch up with him to attach the leash to his color. As they started down the corridor, Casey realized this was the way she had walked the other morning when she had seen JR in the hallway.

"Hmm…you don't think…" Casey paused.

"What?"

"Just had a thought, but I want to ask my mom a quick question before we walk."

Casey poked her head in the office and said, "Mom, what unit does Mrs. Kelly live in?"

"She's in 204."

Casey's eyes widened, and she nodded at Matt to leave.

"What's up?"

Casey's eyes stared at the ground. "I don't like what I'm thinking."

"Well, let's hear it anyway." Matt responded.

Chester began tugging at the leash and the two started walking.

Her mom stuck her head out the door, "Here's a bag in case you need it for Chester clean up."

"I forgot about that part of the job," Casey sighed.

"Quit keeping me in suspense. I can hear the wheels turning in that head of yours. Let's have it," Matt said.

The Colors of the Sea

"When I delivered a package for my mom the other morning, I walked down the same corridor we were just on for Chester. I noticed JR bending down to pick up something, but I didn't think anything of it. Now I find out that it was right in front of Mrs. Kelly's apartment. Knowing that Mrs. Swenson kept a key out there, I can't help but wonder if Mrs. Kelly hid one also."

Matt stared at Casey. "You don't really think JR would steal that money do you?"

"I sure hope not. But it is a pretty strange coincidence. What would possess people to leave a key outside their door anyway?"

"I guess they lock themselves out and don't want it to happen again," Matt replied. "I know my mom hides one on a ledge inside our garage. It is hidden so that you would never see it, but it is pretty common I think."

"Mrs. Schmitt I can almost understand, because she is such a grouch; but Mrs. Kelly is such a sweet lady. I can't imagine that JR would want to bother her."

"Maybe you should tell JR what you saw."

"I'm not afraid of JR, but I don't know what he'd think about some younger kids accusing him of stealing. I know I'm not ready to say anything to my mom or dad yet.

"Mr. Kearns likes JR. Maybe we should discuss it with him."

"I think that's a good idea." Casey sighed. "I was really starting to feel better about JR. I'm almost sorry I noticed him stopping there."

"Well, you certainly can't feel bad about that. This stealing thing has to stop. It isn't great for the publicity of the Blue Heron, let alone everything else." Matt reassured her. "I don't think you can ignore it."

"You're right," Casey agreed. "Yuck," Casey added as she picked up the neat little package Chester had dropped along the sidewalk. "This is the only part I don't like about dogs."

Chapter 8

Charles Kearns sat in the shade of the picnic table with his paints, trying to get enough energy to carry his easel and supplies out to the beach. He saw Casey and Matt walking toward him and noticed that they looked unusually serious.

"If I were painting you two this morning, I'd have to use shades of gray and black," Mr. Kearns said, "You looked troubled."

"You're reading us right," Casey said.

"Sounds serious."

"It's something I'd like to ignore, but I can't. At the same time, I don't want to accuse someone of something that they didn't do."

"Go on," the gentle voice encouraged.

Casey took a deep breath. "The morning of the last robbery, I saw JR bend down and, I think pick up something in front of Mrs. Kelly's door. I'm wondering if she had hidden a key, and if JR used it."

"That is serious," Mr. Kearns said.

"We know we should talk to JR, but we were hoping maybe you would help us. We know he likes you. We're not sure what his reaction would be to us. It might make him pretty mad."

"Now is as good a time as any. Here he comes on his daily trek down to the beach with his detector."

Mr. Kearns motioned to JR to join them. JR looked extremely tired. He took a deep breath and slowly approached the table.

"What's up?" JR asked.

Casey and Matt here think you might have a problem you need help working out."

"Is that right?" JR looked at the two children who looked pretty unhappy themselves.

"I'm sorry, JR. I don't want to cause you any trouble. I know you hate being here, and I can understand that perfectly. But the problem is, I thought I saw you pick up something in front of Mrs. Kelly's door the morning of the robbery, and I couldn't help wondering about it."

"I don't remember seeing you," JR stared out at the shimmering water.

"I was running an errand for my mom and had just come around the corner of the stairwell."

"If you have a problem JR, four heads here are better than one," Mr. Kearns encouraged.

"Oh, I have a humongous problem all right," JR retorted. "I've done some pretty stupid things in my life, but this time..." JR's voice became husky with emotion.

"It's that old witch, Mrs. Schmitt. Every time I walk past her unit, which I am forced to do every time I leave the building, she has to make a rotten comment. 'JR, turn down the radio. JR, you need a haircut. JR, why does your aunt let you dress in those ripped cutoffs with such big holes.' I try to sneak past her door, but she is a hawk... waiting patiently, staring, and ready to attack."

"Well, I thought I was the only one she didn't approve of in the neighborhood," Mr. Kearns chuckled.

"Well, that is part of my problem. No one bothers to talk to me here, except you, although Casey, Matt, and Cory have tried. I haven't made any friends because everyone comes and goes so fast, and there really aren't kids my age living here. My parents dumped me in Seniorville. No offense meant..."

"None taken, but I'm not understanding this. Why is that part of your problem?"

"Never mind, I can't go through with this," JR started to bolt from the table, but he felt a firm hand on his shoulder.

"Come on JR...I know it's tough, but let's hear it," Mr. Kearns encouraged.

JR took a deep breath. "The morning before you fixed Mrs. Schmitt's plumbing, I happened to be walking by with my metal detector on. I swung it near the flower pot outside her door, and discovered her key. When I knew she was gone to the theater, I made sure no one was looking and went inside. I saw her petty cash in a jar and thought, 'Good, maybe this will upset her and she'll think about something besides terrorizing me for awhile. I felt pretty good when I heard her scream; but I had no idea that you would be in her apartment that day, or that she'd get to bad mouth you. You're like the only person who tried to be nice to me, and now she was having a great time picking on you. That wasn't exactly what I had in mind."

"Believe me, it's not the first time she's been on my case," Mr. Kearns said. "But what about the other incident? Surely Mrs. Kelly wasn't giving you any grief."

"No, she's never done anything to me. I just used the detector to find another key, and waited until you were in plain view of a lot of people. I watched for Mrs. Kelly to go out. That way even Mrs. Schmitt would have to admit you probably didn't have anything to do with the first one. Great strategy, huh? No one ever said I was smart."

Mr. Kearns couldn't help but smile. "Well JR, the real you must have come out in the second situation, otherwise you wouldn't have tried to clear my name."

There were tears in JR's eyes, and he looked embarrassed. "I can't believe I got myself into such a mess."

"Do you still have the money, or did you spend it?" Casey asked.

"Yeah, I still have it. I've been trying to figure out what to do. Tell you the truth, Casey, I'm almost relieved that you saw me and were smart enough to put two and two together. I'm tired of not sleeping at night. My aunt is going to freak out, that is for sure. I don't even want to think about my parents."

"I think we can do some damage control," Mr. Kearns smiled. "Let's go talk to a few people."

JR shocked Casey and Matt as he reached out to shake hands with them. "You guys are all right. You could have run to the police, Mrs. Schmitt, or my aunt instead of trying to confront me. I'm sure that wasn't easy. Thanks."

Matt stood there and shook his head as Mr. Kearns and JR walked toward his aunt's apartment. "Well, that went pretty well."

"I feel sorry for him. Hopefully it will work out okay."

Casey could tell when she walked in the office that a new problem was in the air. Her mom looked very worried.

"The tropical depression that we've been watching has turned into a named storm. It could become a category one hurricane, but they don't expect it to get any stronger than that. We have a lot of prep work to do around here. We still have about thirty-six hours to get ready, and we're going to need it."

"So much for being caught up," Casey's dad said, "I need to get the office windows boarded, and you three can start looking for any loose items around the complex that could turn into missiles. I'm sure some of the residents would appreciate your help in moving plants off their lanais. We can leave some lounge chairs out for another twenty-four hours so the residents can still use them, but I am going to start moving most of them into the storage unit."

A few hours later, Kerry Simms returned to the office. "I've got our supply of batteries for the radio, and I went to the store and bought drinking water and food supplies in case we lose power. Everyone had the same idea. The stores were packed, and some of the shelves were empty. It's hard to know how to decide between what you really need and not be too greedy for the next person."

"I'm scared," Cory whimpered.

"Don't worry, Cory. We're just taking precautions," his dad said calmly.

Casey couldn't get over how the sky was so blue, and how the day looked so normal. In Illinois, if you got any warning about a tornado, it was last minute. All you could do was go to the basement and wait for the radio to tell you that it was safe to go upstairs.

By the end of the next day, everyone was exhausted from all the activity. The planters that weren't stationary had been moved, boards had been applied to the windows without shutters, and all the loose items that could be picked up and stored had been removed.

"Am I seeing right?" Casey asked.

"What?" Matt responded.

"Is that really JR and Mr. Kearns helping Mrs. Schmitt move her plants inside."

"No way!" Casey exclaimed and shook her head. "We've been so busy that I haven't had a chance to talk to Mr. Kearns or JR."

"I can't decide if this is easier or harder to deal with than Illinois tornadoes. You have time to prepare for a hurricane, but a lot more time to worry about it too."

"I don't suppose anyone likes either," Matt added.

"Tell them that," Casey said and pointed to the boogey board riders and a few surfboarders who were delighted with the increase in wave activity at the beach. She had never seen the waves crash as hard as they were this morning. They watched as the surf and paddleboarders tumbled in the waves as they crashed over them. It didn't seem to bother them. They just picked up their board and started paddling back to do it again.

"They sure are having fun! I wish I could try that, but I am not sure I am brave enough yet. Maybe someday…." Casey said. She looked up at the sky which was changing color.

Casey paused, "Mr. Kearns would probably say the color of the sea is sap green and burnt umber!"

"Get ready for grey," Matt added. "I need to go home and make sure my mom doesn't need any more help. She hates storms. When she was young, her home had a lot of damage. Just the sound of the wind reminds her of how frightened she was. I guess it was bad enough she can never forget it. I'll see you after the storm. The feeder bands will be starting soon."

Chapter 9

During the night, Casey heard the rain start. The wind didn't seem that bad, and it just seemed like a regular storm. There wasn't much lightning, and it didn't even seem as bad as a typical Florida thunderstorm. Some of the lightning storms she had witnessed since she had been in Florida had been amazing to her. "Tampa is the lightning capital of the world," her dad had told her. She definitely believed that, especially when you watched the electric show out over the water.

By morning the winds had picked up, and the whole family found that they were glued to the weather news on the television. The storm was approaching the 75mph Category one status, but the main concerns were still flooding from the expected six inches of rain and beach erosion. The winds were getting strong, but the condo felt secure. Casey was glad that she didn't live on a higher floor, although if there were a storm surge she realized she might feel differently. The queen palms were swaying and bowing quite low to the ground. Rain pelted sideways, and it looked like an aluminum gutter had blown off the end of one of the units. "That's it, away from door, and back to the shuttered room," Mr. Simms ordered.

The lights flickered several times during the morning and finally went out.

Casey grabbed the portable radio and turned on the news to find out what was happening.

Power was out for 30,000 residents in the area, and crews were going to start working as soon as the worst of the storm had passed. They hoped that would start happening in an hour or so.

"Monopoly anyone?" Mrs. Simms asked.

"You must be kidding," Casey said.

"We have battery lights, a few candle jars, lots of snacks, and not much else to do right now so why not? When the rain stops, I have a feeling we'll be busy for the next few days. We might as well do something to pass the time."

It felt strange to be playing a game during the storm, but Casey had to admit the next few hours went more quickly. But the waiting was still not easy for anyone. They didn't want to open the refrigerator door, so they settled on peanut butter sandwiches and apples for dinner.

Michael Simms couldn't stand it anymore. He had been pacing the floor for the last hour. "The wind has definitely slowed down, and the rain has stopped for now. I'm sure there will be a few more feeder bands, but I am going to take a look around."

When he returned an hour later, he took off his raincoat and sat down at the kitchen table.

"We lost a few gutters, and a few residents on the top floor complained that the water came under their sliding glass doors. They were keeping up with wet vacs until the power went out. Fortunately, by that the time, the strongest part of the winds had passed. They are going to need extra help to bring in large vacuums and fans to get dried out quickly. Hopefully, they can save the carpets and flooring, and they don't think it got deep enough to get into the wallboard. Midnight Pass is pretty flooded, but not as bad as what they are saying about Casey Key. There was a lot of erosion on Turtle Beach. Basically though, we are in pretty good shape. Lucky for us the storm never reached hurricane strength. The path of the storm moved north so it wasn't as severe here.

Dad said it was safe for Casey and Cory to have a look around the property but not to leave the complex as a few feeder bands were still possible. They put on their ponchos and stepped outside. Palm tree fronds littered the ground. A cabbage palm had fallen completely down next to the street, and a garbage lid was leaning against it. A twisted piece of aluminum gutter had wrapped itself around a palm tree in the courtyard, and various kinds of debris scattered the landscape. They edged closer to the beach. The whitecaps were not as high as they had been in the brownish gray water, but they still crashed noisily against the shore. The ocean looked angry as though it was complaining about the disturbance that had been created in its waters.

"I guess the sea does have a personality after all," Casey thought.

The beach was littered with all types of plant debris that had washed ashore along with many shells and creatures she wasn't used to seeing there.

"I need Mr. Kearns to tell me what some of these are," Casey said as she and Cory gathered a few unknown specimens. It started to rain again, and they ran back to the office.

After several hours, there was a cheer as the electricity came back on. "Good, not long enough to hurt any of the food in the fridge," her mom said.

"I guess I prefer tropical storms," thought Casey as she thought about the aftermath of a tornado she had witnessed once in Illinois. She knew, however, it would not always be that way.

Chapter 10

Four days passed and life at the Blue Heron was getting back to normal. Casey stepped out her front door and gazed at the beach. A deep blue horizon line separated the ocean from the sky, and the sun sparkled in white streaks across the blues and turquoise shaded ocean. She turned toward the parking lot and saw Matt waving at her.

"Quick, you'll want to see this," said Matt. "Mr. Kearns is fishing on the intercoastal side at the pier. He sent me to get you."

"What is it?" Casey asked

"You'll see." Matt responded.

"Good, you made it in time," Mr. Kearns said as they approached.

A water hose bubbled in the water, and it had attracted some special guests. Casey looked into the water and saw two grayish brown shapes. A mother manatee and her baby floated next to the pier.

"I can't believe it," Casey said.

"I had seen Snooty up at the museum in Bradenton but have only seen them here in the intercoastal a few times," Matt said.

"She is so big," said Casey, "and the baby is so cute. Look how close it stays to her mother. They look so gentle. What are those marks on the mother's back?"

"That is a scar from a boat injury," Mr. Kearns responded. "There is another mark on her left side. She is one of the lucky ones. Manatees don't move very quickly. A deep cut could have killed her. Manatees are identified by their various injury markings."

"That's terrible!" Casey exclaimed as she watched the two gentle creatures start to move away from the pier.

"The good news is that one of the adaptations of a manatee is that it heals remarkably fast when it is injured, if it hasn't been a head injury or that it hasn't cut deep into a rib. I'm afraid their numbers are down to less than 3,000 left in our Florida waters. A bad red tide year would not be good for them."

"At least it seems like the storm did something to help get rid of the red tide, Matt noted as they started losing sight of the manatees.

"It does seem to be pretty much gone for now," Mr. Kearns added. He looked at the two children for a few seconds and then said, "JR thought you'd like an update. He's still pretty embarrassed, but thought you deserved to know what has happened." Casey and Matt stared into the gray eyes they had come to admire.

"The money has been returned to both Mrs. Schmitt and Mrs. Kelly. The police are satisfied with letting JR appear at teen court, which will probably give him some community service things to do. The matter will be pretty much settled. His aunt is still upset, but he is trying to make amends to her too. He has been working hard to help clean up the water that came under her sliding glass doors during the storm. She'll get over it, and he'll be headed back north for school at the end of the summer. I know you have both been concerned. You are responsible for really getting JR out of a jam. He wanted me to tell you he appreciates it."

No one spoke for a few minutes as they all were deep in thought. Mr. Kearns broke the silence. "Let's see if I can catch anything for dinner tonight."

Casey and Matt headed back to the beach. They couldn't stop thinking about the series of events that had happened with JR.

"We should have figured out that the metal detector had something to do with it," said Matt.

"Well, as soon as I found out that he felt enough respect for Mr. Kearns to try and clear his name, I couldn't be mad at him anymore," Casey added.

"And at least he hadn't spent any of the money, and he did return the money to its owners," Matt said..

"Do you suppose Mrs. Schmitt apologized to Mr. Kearns," responded Matt.

"Yeah, right," Casey said sarcastically.

When they got back to the office, Cory was sitting on the picnic table watching a great white egret take long slow steps across the lawn as it stalked a lizard. It stopped and its long neck moved forward and back in a fascinating rhythm.

"It reminds me of a Far Eastern dance," Casey laughed, "You know one of those where people move their neck sideways back and forth."

The egret stopped and froze like a statue. Two lizards darted around the palm tree. The male lizard's neck pulsed in and out. When it expanded, it looked like a red balloon.

"He's showing off for his girlfriend," Matt said. "It's a mating call."

Suddenly, the egret struck, and its long- pointed beak pierced its prey.

"Got him," Cory said.

"I never know whether to feel bad for the lizard, or happy for the bird catching his dinner." Casey sighed.

JR had just walked past the picnic table with his metal detector in hand. His gaze had stayed downward, but he paused and turned around after he passed.

"You want to look for treasures today, Cory?"

Cory leaped off the bench and was instantly at JR's side.

Casey met JR's eyes and smiled. "Good hunting," she added.

JR looked relieved, and the odd twosome headed toward the shore.

Walkers headed toward the north end of the key to watch the sunset. Casey and Matt sat down on the shore and watched the sun sink lower in the sky. The sky was ablaze with color. I don't think Mr. Kearns's palette could possibly be large enough to create all the colors here tonight," Casey said. She scanned the sky and picked out various shades of blue, pink, purple, lavender, and orange. The sun touched the horizon and the golden glow spread across the water. The palette of the sky reflected across the water. She knew that in two short minutes the sun would be slip below the horizon, and that more color would burst through in the afterglow shortly after it disappeared.

Matt looked at her and nudged her lightly with his elbow. "Well, is it beginning to feel like home yet?"

Casey watched the gentle waves bob until they splashed and foamed at the shore, touched the land, and then retreated. She realized she had become attached to the sound of the surf and the laughing gulls, and the many moods and colors of the sea.

Casey looked at Matt and smiled as she realized that many days are full of surprises. "Yes," she said, "I guess it is."

www.ingramcontent.com/pod-product-compliance
Ingram Content Group UK Ltd.
Pitfield, Milton Keynes, MK11 3LW, UK
UKHW022219230426
12048UKWH00016BA/951